The Real Adventures of Carly & Sam

Pre-teen Shenanigans Part 1

Written and Illustrated by:

Lucinda Ward

AuthorHouse™
1663 Liberty Drive
Bloomington, IN 47403
www.authorhouse.com
Phone: 1 (800) 839-8640

Because of the dynamic nature of the Internet, any web addresses or links contained in this book may have changed since publication and may no longer be valid. The views expressed in this work are solely those of the author and do not necessarily reflect the views of the publisher, and the publisher hereby disclaims any responsibility for them.

Any people depicted in stock imagery provided by Getty Images are models, and such images are being used for illustrative purposes only.
Certain stock imagery © Getty Images.

This book is printed on acid-free paper.

ISBN: 978-1-7283-4257-3 (sc)
ISBN: 978-1-7283-4256-6 (e)

Library of Congress Control Number: 2020900314

Print information available on the last page.

Published by AuthorHouse 01/08/2020

authorHOUSE®

FOREWORD

As the husband, friend and retired U.S. Army Solider, I've seen Lucinda's love for families, education and most of all children grow at an unprecedented rate. For more than 20 years she has operated in childcare and believes imputing positivity and discipline in children. The chapters within this book are invigorating, funny and most of all lessons learned to all readers, children and adults alike; reflecting many things seen within the 20 plus years.

When Lucinda mentioned she was in thoughts of writing a second book after her first, "I'm Perfect Just the Way I Am ", I wanted to know what angle she would tackle, what the characters would look like and what are the lessons to be learned. After reading "The Real Adventures of Carly and Sam, Pre-Teen Shenanigans Part 1", I can't help but to read the chapters over and over again!

Although this book is geared toward children, I hope it will be read by adults as well. It's a must read for everyone!

Timothy J. Ward Sr.

The Real Adventures of Carly and Sam
Pre–teen Shenanigans Part 1

Contents

Chapter 1 ~ The Almost Wrecked Vacation

Sam and Carly have been friends since they can remember. They were born at the same hospital but on different days, of course. When Carly turned three, her family moved right next door to Sam. Sam's mom said that they would have never known that another kid moved next door if Carly would not have thrown the loudest tantrums known to man. One summer Carly and Sam's parents thought it would be a great idea to build a treehouse in the huge oak tree in the back yard that was half in Carly's backyard and half in Sam's backyard as a surprise secret clubhouse. Carly said that building that clubhouse was the best adult decision her parents have made in her life. Sam felt the same way.

"I can't believe we are going to the Bahamas together," Carly said to Sam as she glared across the fence. "Operation Clubhouse," Sam yelled excitedly.

Immediately, Sam climbed up her ladder in her yard to the treehouse while Carly climbed up the ladder in her yard. Both girls met up in the combined treehouse.

Carly and Sam looked at their calendar and checked off the final day before leaving to go to the Bahamas.

"Sam, we need to go over our packing list," said Carly.

Carly pulled out a small yellow sheet of paper from her right shoe. As she unfolded the old paper, Carly began to name off items;

"Swim Suit, check"

"Fidget Spinner, check"

"Favorite Baseball Cap, check"

"IPad, check"

"Nintendo DS, check"

"Diary, check"

"This is going to be the best vacation ever," said Sam.

The next morning Sam, her dad, her mom and her baby sister headed to the airport to meet Carly and her mom for the best vacation known to a nine-year-old.

Carly's dad was in the Army and was deployed to Kuwait. It had been almost a year since he first left and going on summer trips is his favorite thing to do with her. Carly was excited and ready to get on the plane.

Sam's family met Carly and her mom at the front entrance of the airport. Carly struggled as she pulled her medium size, pink, Hello Kitty luggage up to the counter in front of the ticket agent with her left hand while clenching her favorite Wonder woman backpack with her right hand.

"Hi, little lady," the agent said as she pulled Carly's bag onto the rotating belt. Carly looked up at the beautiful agent and excitement took over her entire body. Pressing her cheeks into her hands as she leaned up against the ticket counter, barely able to reach the top, Carly rambled, "Hi. Wow, you are really pretty! You look like you can be an Instagram model. Do you have an Instagram? I'm going to keep my backpack. I'm going to the Bahamas, you know. Have you been there? I bet it's dreamy..."

"I know you are excited but let the nice lady do her job," Carly's mom said as she placed her hand on Carly's shoulder and squeezed tightly. Carly looked up and saw her mom's death stare piercing through her face. Carly immediately stopped talking but proceeded to twiddle her thumbs and pace back and forth.

The agent bent across the counter and handed Carly a boarding pass and said, "Gate 21B is where you will board the plane." With a huge grin on her face, Carly snatched the boarding pass out of the agent's hand and held it up to her nose to smell it.

"Sam, look! I have my boarding pass and it says Freeport, Bahamas on it. It just got real!" Carly said.

Sam looked at the ticket agent with puppy dog eyes and a sad face and asked, "Can I please go next to get my boarding pass? I want mines to say Freeport, Bahamas just like Carly's."

The agent gave Sam a full smile and nodded yes. "Do you have any bags, little lady?"

"No, all I have is my backpack," Sam exclaimed as she turned around so the agent can see her bright yellow neon denim backpack. Hanging from the zipper was a black tag with her name, phone number and address embroidered on it.

The agent handed Sam her boarding pass and told both girls to have a safe trip. Carly and Sam skipped excitedly through the airport holding hands and reading each gate sign they passed. Finally, there it was, Gate 21B. The smell of every type of food you could think of filled the area around the gate. Sam and Carly jumped up and down, turned back to their parents and said, "We found it, we found it. Gate 21B. Yayyy. We're going to the Bahamas, We're going to the Bahamas."

Carly and Sam sat at the gate comparing the articles in their backpacks and making sure their packing list from the club house was in there. Sam's mom always told the girls to pack a change of clothes and their toothbrush just in case the bags got lost.

"We will now start boarding flight 9087 to Freeport, Bahamas. We are now boarding seats 1–30," said a very deep voice over the intercom system.

Carly and Sam looked at their tickets. Carly's seat number was 18J and Sam's seat number was 21H.

Carly said, "Mom, I have to poo poo."

"You can poo poo on the plane. You do this every plane ride. You will be ok," Carly's mom said as she gently nudged her closer to the terminal tunnel.

"It's ok, Carly. I will sit by you. You don't have to be scared," Sam said.

Sam held Carly's hand as they walked through the long tunnel and onto the plane. As people entered the plane, Sam noticed that Carly was not acting her normal hyper self. She could not understand why Carly was acting so strangely especially since she already went poo poo and drank all of her little sister's apple juice. She wondered what was going on.

"Good morning ladies and gentlemen. I am Bahama Mama and I will be your captain today. Please fasten your seat belts as we prepare to depart," the captain said.

Sam looked over at Carly. She was fast asleep with her mouth and one eye open and her head propped up on her mom's shoulder. It looked a little creepy. Sam got the ipad out of her backpack and started to play Subway Surfers. As soon as she collected 10,000 coins she could see Carly squirming and hear her groaning in her sleep. Then, suddenly, it happened. Carly's head popped straight up and her one closed eye popped open. She pulled at her seat belt and tried to get up in a hurry.

"I got to poo poo again, mom. Move over Sam," Carly yelled out in a demanding voice.

Passengers in the rows in front of Carly turned around to see what all the fuss was about. Carly continued to move but her shoelace was caught in the seat anchor on the floor. Carly's patience was dwindling.

"Mom, do something, hurry," Carly begged as large tears dripped down her rosy cheeks.

Carly's mom bent over and tried very hard to untangle the shoelace. Just then she got the surprise of a lifetime.

Hesitatingly, Carly put both hands on her bottom.

BRUMMMMPPPPP! A loud noise came from seat number 18J followed by the sound of whimpering and the smell of sewer.

"Oh no," Carly's mom said as she looked at Carly's saggy pants. She grabbed Carly's backpack and proceeded to rush her to the bathroom.

"Excuse me ma'am. You must remain seated and put on your seat belt so we can depart," said the flight attendant walking towards Carly's mom. As she got closer her face started to frown and she placed her hand over her nose.

"What is that horrific smell?" said the flight attendant.

Carly and her mom continued to fast walk up the narrow aisle and into the bathroom. Carly's mom helped Carly get out of the poop pants and get cleaned up. The smell filled the airplane like a cloud hovering over a cool body of water. The flight attendant picked up the receiver from the wall and told the captain that the flight might need to be delayed a few minutes because there was a slight problem with the passenger occupying seat 18J. As soon as the flight attendant hung up the receiver, there was another message over the intercom system.

"Attention passengers! This is Captain Bahama Mama. We are experiencing a delay in our take off due to minor complications on board. Please remain seated as we continue to get the situation under control," said the captain.

Carly's mom searched Carly's backpack for the change of clothes she was asked to pack. The clothes were nowhere to be found. The backpack was full of toys and books. Carly's mom began to think about what she was going to do about getting a change of underwear, pants and socks for Carly. As Carly's mom leaned against the sink to think, the flight attendant knocked on the door and whispered, "Are you ok in there, ma'am? Is there anything I can help you with?"

"I don't have a change of clothes for my daughter. They are in her checked baggage," said Carly's mom.

"Ok ma'am I may have something that can help. I'll be right back," said the flight attendant.

About 20 seconds later, the flight attendant came back to the door. She knocked twice and said, "Ma'am, I have two blankets and four safety pins you can use. Use one blanket and two safety pins to make a diaper panties for her and the other blanket and safety pins like a skirt on top of the diaper panties."

Carly's mom slowly opened the door, stuck her hand out to get the blankets and pins and said thank you as she closed the door.

Five minutes later, Carly opened the bathroom door and stepped out. She had a relieved yet apologetic look on her face. As she walked down the narrow istle, she can hear the faint whispers and see the passengers admiring her unique outfit. Carly's mom made a purple and grey airline blanket look like a stylish sarong. Carly smiled at the staring eyes and gave a well-prepared Miss America wave all the way back to seat 18J. The flight to the Bahamas was a smooth one.

"Ladies and gentlemen, we are about to land. Please make sure all seat belts are fastened and remain seated until the seat belt signs turn off," said the flight attendant over the intercom.

As soon as the plane landed, Carly hopped up to stretch. All the passengers moved out of the way and let Carly and her mom get off of the plane first. Carly stepped off the plane and walked through the long tube before reaching the airport. Carly's mom noticed two beautiful brown skin women dressed in long floral print dresses. They both had pink flowers in their hair. One was holding a sign that read "Carly." The other was holding a large wooden platter. On the platter was a stack of clothing and three small bottles.

Carly's mom guided Carly to the two women.

"You must be Carly," said the woman holding the sign.

"Yes, I am," said Carly.

"Compliments of the airline for your Bahama vacation we would like to give you this gift. It is a change of clothes, shampoo, conditioner, and body wash," said the woman holding the platter.

Carly reached out and took the clothes off the platter. She grinned ear to ear and thanked both women.

"And to think, this was the almost wrecked vacation," said Carly's mom.

Chapter 2 ~ Backyard Mayhem

It was a very rainy Saturday morning. Sam turned the door knob and opened the door that led into Carly's mud room. She was dripping wet from head to toe. As she sat on the old wooden bench, she slowly took off her wet coat and boots.

"Is that you, Sam," yelled Carly down the hallway.

"Yes, it is. I'm in the mudroom taking off my boots," Sam yelled back.

"Stop yelling in this house," screamed Carly's mom.

Carly walked into the mud room and smiled at Sam. She helped her hang up her wet yellow raincoat and place her shiny pink rain boots onto the drying rack. Carly knew that if it was not done correctly her mom would be upset. Carly handed Sam a pair of slippers and the two girls walked into the kitchen. All the while, Sam never looked up at Carly.

"Would you girls like to have a nice cup of hot chocolate?" asked Carly's mom. "Yes," said Carly as she smiled with dancing eyes. Sam simply nodded her head in an up and down motion without saying a word. She did not even make eye contact with Carly's mom at all.

The girls sat on the tall bar stools at the island waiting for their hot chocolate. There was a dead space of awkward silence that filled the kitchen. "Why are you girls acting so weird this morning? First, you come in here yelling through the house. Then, I notice Sam wearing my favorite house slippers. That never happens. And now, the cat has got both of your tongues. It is so quiet in here that if you drop a coin, the Duke in England would be able to hear the echo. What's really going on?" asked Carly's mom.

Carly looked up at her mom with the saddest, helpless eyes a preteen could ever have. She gave a great big sigh and then looked back down at the marble tile on the island. Sam then looked up at Carly and without hesitation she threw her hands in the air allowing them to freely fall back to her side. Sam grunted and hopped off the bar stool and walked towards the stove where Carly's mom stood stirring the hot chocolate in a tin pot.

"Well, since Carly is too chicken to say anything, I guess I have to step up and be the bigger person here." said Sam.

Carly's mom stopped stirring the pot and turned around to look at Sam. "I'm listening," she said.

Sam took a deep breath. Looking at Carly's mom and speaking very fast Sam blurted out her deepest emotions. "Ok...here goes nothing. It is already April and we have not even planned our celebration for the month. Usually we already have the invitations out by now and we already know what we want to do. I'm afraid that we are getting too old for this. After all, we are preteens. I'm really mad because Carly has no ideas to help us out and all she keeps talking about is how cool the Renaissance Era was. I really do not care about history. All I care about right now is our traditional April celebration. We started this together and now I feel Carly thinks she is too good for it." said Sam.

"Oh, you are talking about the celebration that you girls do every April for Month of the Military Child, right?" asked Carly's mom.

"Yes, that one." Carly murmured under her breath.

Carly's mom sat three small coffee mugs on the island. She asked the girls to be careful because the hot chocolate was hot and placed one handful of colored miniature marshmallows in each mug. She slid two of the mugs over to the girls. Once again awkward silence filled the room.

"Well, I think Carly gave you a perfect idea, Sam. Have you thought about doing a Renaissance fair or a Viking vs. Knight celebration?" Asked Carly's mom as she confidently lifted her coffee mug and walked out of the room.

"That's it, Carly. We will do a Viking vs. Knight celebration. We will send out invitations right away to all the neighborhood kids to come dressed as a Knight or a Viking." Sam exclaimed excitedly.

"Sam! That's a perfect idea for a perfect celebration. We could even have a jousting match," said Carly.

Satisfied with the celebration idea, the girls hugged each other and headed to Carly's room to work on the invitations. As they walked down the hallway, they continued to blurt out ideas to each other. Smiles covered their faces as the silence faded and instant preteen babbling voices filled the house.

"Make sure to put my slippers back when you pass the mud room," yelled Carly's mom from the living room.

"Stop yelling in this house," yelled Carly and Sam back to Carly's mom while chuckling at the same time.

Carly and Sam worked for three hours straight on fliers and invitations for the Viking vs. Knight Celebration. On the front of the invitation was a picture of a Viking on the left and a knight on the right and Carly and Sam in the middle. On the inside left side of the invitation read;

Hear ye, Hear ye

Come one, come all to the spectacular Viking vs. Knight Celebration.

When: Saturday, April 11 from 12:00 o'clock until 2:00 o'clock

Where: 1857 Shady Green Pickle Road

Special Instructions: Must come dressed as either a Viking or a knight to participate in the celebration.

On the right side of the invitation was a collage of pictures that represented Vikings and knights. It looked like a Where's Waldo page but in a cool way.

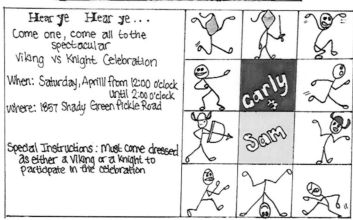

Carly and Sam were proud of their invitations and could not wait to start handing them out. Besides, the celebration was set for the next Saturday and time was getting short.

The girls gathered their invitations and separated them between two backpacks. They both put on their backpacks and headed outside. The rain had stopped, and it was perfect weather to hand out invitations. Carly hopped onto her bike and Sam hopped on her scooter.

"I'll go left and hand out invitations on all these streets before we get to the freeway while you go right and hand out invitations on all the streets before you get to the Middle School. Is that a deal?" asked Sam.

"Sure! Let's do this. See you later," said Carly.

After an hour and a half, the girls met back at Carly's house. All 75 of the invitations were handed out. For the next five days, Carly and Sam worked hard getting the celebration together. They made several trips back and forth to the grocery store and party store with Sam's mom. The girls did not seem to mind because all they wanted was for this celebration to be amazing.

Finally, Saturday, April 11 arrived. The scene in Sam's backyard was epic. In the front yard was a sign that read "WELCOME VIKINGS & KNIGHTS. COME AROUND BACK." Dividing the backyard was a long table that sat 52 people. It was really several tables put together in a straight line with burlap fabric placed on top as a tablecloth. Plastic gold jeweled wine goblets, silver plastic plates, and gold plastic forks were at each place setting. A basket of bread was in the middle of the table after every fourth setting. There were three colorful Raj tents on each side of the table. Flag banners with the Medieval crest hung from the tops of the tents to the tree house. Sam's back door was transformed into a castle drawbridge door. On the right side of the door stood a six-foot black knight cut-out. On the left side of the door stood a six-foot Viking cut-out. Carly's dad made a look alike castle surrounding the door with cardboard boxes, paint, and a lot of tape. Carly's dad even placed a stockade next to a fake boulder that was very realistic. Carly was dressed as a knight and Sam was dressed as a Viking. Their costumes were very realistic considering they made them from supplies they collected around the neighborhood.

"I hear someone trying to get into the gate. I think we have our first guest," said Sam excitedly.

Carly ran over to the gate with Sam. With huge grins on their faces, they opened the gate together. Much to their surprise, it wasn't just a guest, it was about 35 guests at the same time.

"Welcome to the Vikings vs. Knights Celebration," said Carly.

The guests pushed past Carly and Sam at the back gate and ran into the back yard. A great deal of oohs and awws came out of their mouths. They could not believe the incredible decorations. After a few minutes of taking it all in, there was a trumpet sound. All the guests froze and looked around. No one knew where the sound came from. The trumpet sounded again. This time all the guests turned and faced the back door. It was Carly's dad blowing the trumpet to get everyone's attention.

"Wow, that's genius," said one guest dressed in a Viking costume.

"Hear ye, hear ye Vikings and Knights! Smoked turkey legs and boiled potatoes for everyone!" he said.

All the guests cheered and rushed over to the table to eat.

"Don't eat too much because we have games planned for everyone to join in, but you will lose if you are lazy because you ate too much," said Sam.

"Yeah, don't be a fatty," said Carly.

"Be nice," said Carly's dad.

As the guests ate, more and more guests entered the back yard with the same reaction as the first group. After a few minutes the trumpet sounded again. Sam's dad and a few of the neighbors came walking through the back gate with a large rectangular platform. As they walked closer to the table, Sam noticed some of the neighbors holding equipment in their hands. Carly's dad began to speak,

"Hear ye, hear ye. We are about to start our first competition of the day. For this competition we seek out the bravest and most skilled competitor. I will need one knight and one Viking for this competition. This competition is called JOUSTING."

"I'll represent the Vikings," said Sam as she ran over to Carly's dad.

The neighbors put the rectangular platform on the ground. It was a slightly bouncy stage that looked like a wrestling ring without the outside ropes.

One of the neighbors walked over to Sam and handed her a red padded jousting lance.

"I feel sorry for the knight that goes against me because you are about to get crushed," said Sam.

"I'll verse you," said a voice by the back gate.

All eyes turned toward the gate to see who the mysterious competitor was. It was Jake Snider. Jake has been Carly's big time crush since the first grade. Jake was also the person that Sam disliked the most in all the world.

"Bring it on then, Jake," said Sam.

"No, I want to verse him!" said Carly as she ran to the neighbor to get a jousting lance.

"Back up Carly and let me defeat the beast," said Sam.

Carly grabbed the blue jousting lance and pointed it at Sam. Carly kept her eye on Sam while walking backwards towards the stage. Carly hopped up on the stage and Sam followed. With a great deal of enthusiasm and excitement, the guests watched Sam and Carly closely. Sam and Carly went back and forth hitting each other with the jousting lances while talking about Jake. Sam continued to talk about how big of a fake he was while Carly kept shouting how amazing he and his hair was.

"STOP IT RIGHT NOW! This is a party not WWE. What is this all about anyway?" yelled Carly's mom.

"Jake," said Carly and Sam together.

As soon as Jake heard his name he begin to tip toe towards the back gate with his head down.

"Stop, Jake," yelled Sam.

Jake started walking quickly as soon as he heard is name. Carly looked at Sam and both girls dropped their jousting lances.

"Get him," said Carly as she pointed towards Jake.

Jake started to run at full speed out of the back yard. A crowd full of guests dressed in Viking and Knight costumes chased Jake down the street.

Tears ran down Jake's cheeks as he screamed, "Mama" between pants for air. Around the corner was a park. As soon as the crowd reached the park they stopped to catch their breath.

"I think we scared him good enough," said Sam.

"Yeah, let's go home," said Carly.

"Best Month of the Military Child party mayhem ever," said a guest.

Carly and Sam gave each other a high five and smiled as they walked back to the house.

The Unexpected B.B.Q.

Chapter 3 ~ The Unexpected Barbecue

Sam and Carly sat quietly in their treehouse looking at each other. A bead of sweat ran down Sam's forehead onto her eyelid. It was the second week of June and Sam and Carly could not decide what to do. Besides the fact that it was already 92 degrees at 10:30 a.m., Sam and Carly had already played hop–scotch, rode their bikes around the neighborhood, and updated their Instagram stories. Suddenly, the sound of the creaking of the backyard fence captured the attention of the girls. Sam and Carly quickly crawled over to the treehouse window and peeked their heads out. Down below was Carly's dad with a leash. Carly's dad slowly opened the fence.

"Whatcha got there, daddy?" asked Carly.

"I have a temporary house guest. You girls should come down and see," Carly's dad replied.

As Carly's dad continued to slowly walk into the backyard. Sam and Carly climbed down the treehouse ladder. Tugging at the leash, Carly's dad walked a medium size goat through the fence.

Sam's face lit up like candles on a birthday cake. Her eyes opened wide, she placed her hand over her mouth, and took two steps back and hid behind Carly.

"No way, dad. Where did you get it from. How long do we get to keep it?" asked Carly.

"Carly, I got this little fellow from Santos Farm across town. He will be with us for about a month. He will be gone right before we have our traditional 4th of July Bar–B–Q," Carly's dad answered.

Carly's dad walked the goat over to the big tree in the middle of the yard. He connected the leash to an already existing rope that was on the tree. Carly walked over with her dad to the tree while Sam watched from the backyard fence.

"Sam, come over and pet him. Why are you all the way over there?" asked Carly.

"I think I will stay right here, just in case he gets loose and I have to run," replied Sam.

Carly and her dad laughed at Sam's comment and Carly continued to pet the goat.

"Dad, what's his name?" asked Carly.

"I don't think he has one," said Carly's dad.

"Well, we will call him Billy. As in Billy the Goat!" said Carly snickering to herself.

"You hear that, Sam? His name is Billy. As in Billy the Goat," Carly yelled across the yard.

Sam shook her head and laughed quietly to herself. Carly's dad smiled and finished tying the knot for the leash. Carly went back and forth petting the goat and playing in the treehouse all day long while Sam continued to refuse to pet the goat and just watched from far far away.

The next morning Carly woke up at her usual 9:15 a.m. time. She laid in her bed

thinking about what she wanted to do that day. Then, she remembered that there

was a goat tied up to her tree in the backyard. Carly jumped up out of her bed and ran to the bathroom. She ran her toothbrush under the water and then shoved it into her mouth without any toothpaste. She ran back into her room, picked up a pair of jean shorts off of her floor and sprayed it with fabric refresher. She put on a shirt that was in the basket of clothes shoved in her closet her mom asked her to put away a week ago. She put on her shorts and slid her feet into a pair of flip flops and skipped to the kitchen.

"Good morning, mom," Carly said to her mom who was standing at the kitchen counter pulling a piece of bread out of the toaster.

"Well someone is awfully chipper this morning," said Carly's mom.

"Can't talk now, mom. I have to go see about the goat," said Carly.

Carly opened the pantry door and grabbed the Cheerios box. She shook the open end of the box into a bowl. Then grabbed a handful of Cheerios and placed them in each of her jean shorts pockets. She went in the back yard and fed the Cheerios to Billy the Goat.

Billy the Goat quickly ate the Cheerios out of Carly's hand. Carly looked down at her hand and saw a puddle of saliva dripping from her hand.

"That's disgusting Billy. You didn't have to drool all over my hand," Carly said as she wiped her hands onto the back of her jean shorts.

"Maa," bleated Billy the Goat.

Sam walked into the backyard as Carly finished feeding Billy Cheerios. Sam stood by the backyard fence and did not move. Carly looked over at Sam and waved.

"Hi Sam. Can you bring me a bowl of water for Billy, please," Carly asked.

"Ok. Where is the bowl?" Sam asked.

"It's in the front yard by the water hose," replied Carly.

Sam walked to the front yard. The bowl was exactly where Carly said it would be. Sam turned on the water hose and filled up the bowl. She walked back to the backyard and stopped at the fence.

"Here ya go, Carly," she yelled from the fence.

"It's for Billy. Bring it here, Sam," said Carly.

"Nope. I said I would get water for him. Not bring it to him," replied Sam.

"Oh my goodness, Sam, you are such a chicken," Carly said as she walked towards the back fence. Carly got the bowl of water and walked it over to Billy the Goat sitting it down on the grass next to the tree. Carly noticed that Billy's rope looked like it was worn out. Carly knew that the rope had been there a while but it was in good condition.

"Sam can you go call my dad, please. I want to show him this rope," said Carly.

Minutes later Carly's dad came outside. He was dressed in a pair of blue and green plaid pajama pants with a solid blue robe on top and a pair of slippers. Carly looked him up and down and shook her head. She grabbed his hand and led him to the rope.

"Look dad," she said pointing to the rope.

"Why is it like this? It wasn't like this before," she said.

Carly's dad inspected the rope. First, he held it in his hand. Then, he smelled it. Next, he looked at all sides of the rope.

"Looks like Mr. Billy the Goat has been chewing away at his rope."

Billy the Goat could smell the remains of Cheerios in Carly's pockets. He continued to smell and chew at Carly's jean shorts. Each time Carly inched back, Billy crept forward aiming for her pockets.

"Carly, come up here so you can play a game of Connect Four with me," yelled Sam from the treehouse window.

"Ok I'm coming," yelled Carly as she turned and ran towards the treehouse.

Just at that moment Carly's dad was trying to tighten up the rope. Billy the Goat darted after Carly. Carly's dad lost grip of the rope and Billy was right on Carly's heels. Carly looked behind her and let out a loud fearful squeal. She hopped onto the fourth stair of the treehouse ladder from two feet away. Her heart was beating extremely fast and her legs were legs felt like jello. Once she got up to the treehouse she looked down from the window and noticed that Billy the Goat was nowhere to be found.

"Where did he go," asked Carly.

"He ran out the yard," said Sam.

"Well, how did he manage to open the fence," asked Carly.

"I think I kinda sorta might have not closed it when I went to go get your dad," said Sam.

Carly rolled her eyes at Sam and let out a huge sigh.

"There he is Carly," said Sam pointing out of the treehouse window.

Billy the Goat was trotting in the middle of the street. Carly's dad was not too far behind him holding a rope in his hand.

"Come back here you silly goat," he yelled.

Mr. Overton was Sam's next door neighbor. He knew about all the juicy gossip in the neighborhood. He was known for sitting on his porch and people watching 18 out of 24 hours of the day. Mr. Overton came out when he heard Carly's dad calling Billy the Goat.

"You need some help?" he asked Carly's Dad.

"Yes, please," said Carly's dad.

Mr. Overton and Carly's dad ran down the middle of the street yelling Billy's name. They came to Candy Washington's house at the corner of the street. Candy was the most popular athletic girl in John Oarhnn Middle School. She had shiny long brown hair and enough sass to tame an army. There Candy stood on the sidewalk. She appeared to be taking a selfie with one hand and the other hand was on her hip.

"If you are looking for the goat, he's in there," she said as she pointed to her yard.

"How did you get him in the yard," asked Mr. Overton.

"I was out here sitting on my steps, minding my own business, face timing with my grannie in Maryland, when the goat come trotting in here like he live here. He started eating mama's magnolias and I slipped out the fence and closed him in. I was gonna call mama and tell her not to come out as soon as I got off the phone with grannie but you here now so I ain't gotta do all that," explained Candy.

Mr. Overton and Carly's dad opened the fence and went inside the yard. Carly's dad leaped onto Billy the Goat's back wrapping his arms around his neck.

"Mr. Overton, put the rope around his neck, HURRY!" said Carly's dad.

Mr. Overton rushed over to Billy the Goat and placed the rope around his neck. He pulled it tightly to make sure Billy the Goat was secure.

"I think we are good," he said looking at Carly's dad.

Carly's dad slowly slid off Billy the Goat's back. He grabbed the rope from Mr. Overton and started walking out of Candy's yard.

"You welcome," Candy said in a sassy voice.

"Thank you for helping us," said Carly's dad.

Mr. Overton rolled his eyes at Candy.

"What you need is a whoopin' not a thank you," said Mr. Overton as he followed Carly's dad.

Mr. Overton and Carly's dad walked Billy the Goat back to Carly's house. Carly's dad tied him to the tree just like he did the first time. Carly and Sam watched from the treehouse.

For the next couple of weeks things did not feel the same for Carly. Carly's mom and dad were making lots of calls and inviting people over for dinner. They even invited Candy Washington's family. Carly knew that her dad was a little upset about having to chase Billy the Goat around the neighborhood but did not know what exactly was going on.

Carly's dad had the barbecue grill going all morning. The smell of hickory filled the air. Little by little families from the neighborhood started showing up in Carly's backyard. Mr. Overton bought over his famous homemade macaroni and cheese. Candy Washington bought over a summer fruit salad. There was so much food and everyone was having a great time.

"Dad, it's not the fourth of July yet so why does it seem like we are celebrating?" asked Carly.

"We are having a friendship day," explained Carly's dad.

"That's super fun and nice. Where did you move Billy the Goat?" asked Carly.

Carly's dad stopped barbecuing and looked Carly in her eyes.

"Carly, baby, Billy the Goat is the meat on the grill," said Carly's dad.

Carly looked over at Sam who was sitting at one of the backyard tables. Sam had a plate in front of her stacked with food and Billy the Goat slices were on top.

"I think I am going to have to keep this secret," Carly whispered to her dad.

Carly's dad blurted out a loud laugh and said, "Well, that's what I call an unexpected barbecue".

Chapter 4 ~ Hiking Frenzy

The day had finally arrived. It was camping weekend! Carly and Sam stood at the RV waiting for all the bags to be loaded into the trailer. This RV was special. It was a retirement gift for Sam's dad. He always wanted a camper to go camping so Sam's mom bought him a 2020 Thor Freedom Elite 22FE Camper.

It had a little kitchen with a refrigerator and stove, a couch that lets out into a queen size bed, closet, bathroom with a shower and bunk beds. This special camper could sleep four people. Carly liked it because it had built in wifi and a flat screen television.

"I can't wait to get into our hotel on wheels," said Sam's mom.

"We should be on the road about 4:30 a.m. as soon as Carly's dad finishes loading their camping ear into the trailer," said Sam's dad.

The trailer was attached to a hitch on the back of the camper. It was full of

camping gear and ice chests.

"We got everything in. Let's ride," said Carly's dad.

Carly's family and Sam's family hopped into the RV camper and headed to the campsite.

"Dad, where are we going again," asked Sam.

"We are heading to my favorite campground called Ruidoso. My dad would bring me and your Uncle David here every year. That is why I love camping so much," said Sam's dad.

"You can definitely take your time driving because the wifi is real good in here and I can update my Snapchat story," said Carly.

Sam's dad drove the RV camper and Carly's dad rode shotgun. Sam and Carly sat back on the sofa with their phones. Carly's mom and Sam's mom sat across from each other on the small pull out kitchen table. They played several games of cards. Sam's little sister slept most of the ride.

"Aww, we are almost there," said Sam's dad in a raised voice from the front of the RV.

Sam looked out the window. There, on the side of the road, was a large wooden sign sitting on a faded red brick wall. The sign read, Lincoln National Forest.

"Umm, dad, I don't think we are in Ruidoso. The sign I just read said Lincoln not Ruidoso. Are we lost?" asked Sam.

"No, little lady! Ruidoso is a city in New Mexico. Lincoln National Forest is the name of the campground that is in Ruidoso. We are going to set up camp at this campground," explained Sam's dad as he smiled at her in the rearview mirror.

Carly and Sam pressed their noses up against the window. They saw fog hovering over the nearly nonexistent grass. The large ponderosa pine and Douglas-fir trees looked almost 100 feet tall.

"Dad, are we like the only people here? I haven't seen other people. In fact, this campground looks really spooky with the fog and trees and all," said Carly.

"Carly, it is still very early in the morning. It's only 6:38 in the morning. Noone is going to be up at this hour unless they are fishing," answered Sam's mom.

Carly looked at Sam with a very amused face.

"We get to go fishing too? This is turning from spooky to interesting," said Carly.

Sam's dad drove up to a very secluded area. He placed the camper in the park position and turned off the engine. Carly and Sam hopped out of the camper.

"It smells like Christmas out here and is so chilly," said Sam.

"It does smell like Christmas. But, I think that it looks like a scene out of a movie that does not end on a happy note," said Carly.

"Girls, come on over and help us unload the trailer. As soon as we get everything set up, you will be able to venture off and explore," said Sam's mom.

"Venture off and explore nothing. This place looks too spooky to venture off and explore," said Carly under her breath.

The two families worked together to get the tents put up. Carly's family tent was orange with grey lining. Sam's family tent was red with black lining.

Carly's dad looked at Sam's dad and said, "I don't even know why you put up a tent when you can stay in the camper during the night."

"You are right. But that takes away the whole camping experience for me. In fact, let me show you what we used to do when we were younger," explained Sam's dad.

Sam's dad grabbed a few styrofoam cups and motioned for the girls and Carly's dad to follow him. Everyone, including the moms and followed Sam's dad into the woods. They walked over crunchy pine needles. The smell of fresh air filled their lungs. Five minutes later they came to a small stream. Sam's dad stopped and took a deep breath of the fresh forest air. You could see the look of relaxation mixed with boyish excitement in his face. He handed a cup to each person.

"Here guys. When I was younger..." started Sam's dad before he was distracted.

As he looked up, there stood a man staring at them from across the stream. He had on a red flannel shirt with blue jean overalls, tall rubber black boots, and a baseball cap pulled down low enough to only see the bridge of his nose and his enlarged mustache. He stood tall and his arms were folded.

"Well, would you look at here?" said Sam's dad as he pointed across the stream.

Sam squinted her eyes very hard as if that would make her eyesight more keen. But she could not see that far away.

"Who is that, daddy?" asked Sam.

"Forget who that is, let me know if I should start running back to the camper. I'm sorry but if I get there first, I'm locking everyone out because I am not going to die because of this serial killer today," said Carly.

"Carly, stop being so scary. There isn't a serial killers out here. You are just scared. Hush all that noise!" said Carly's mom.

The man started walking across the stream. He took slow steady steps as his boots disappeared into the water the deeper he got. By the time he reached the middle of the stream, the water was near his knees.

"Yeah, there is no need to be afraid at all. I know that smooth walk anywhere. That's Uncle David," said Carly's dad.

"Ray and Todd! Is that you?" yelled Uncle David across the stream as he waved to Sam and Carly's dad.

"Bro, in the flesh," Sam's dad replied.

"You betcha," said Carly's dad.

Uncle David was Sam's dad's younger brother. They were two years apart. He stood six feet three inches tall and was quite handsome. He was an engineer and worked for the government. He traveled all over the country completing million dollar projects. Sam's dad said that he had the best of both worlds because he was a lady's man and a business partner's jackpot. Carly's dad ran up to the edge of the stream and wrapped his arms around Uncle David's chest. Carly and Sam followed. Sam's dad dapped him up first, then the two gave each other a hug.

"Ladies, aren't you going to come give me a hug?" asked Uncle David.

Carly and Sam's moms looked at each other and giggled. Carly's mom began to blush as they walked over to Uncle David and embraced him. Sam's little sister reached for Uncle David. She smiled big as her little hands magically seemed to vanish in his large mustache.

"I see you have the cups. Were you about to fish?" asked Uncle David.

"Yup we sure were but then I was distracted by your entrance," replied Sam's dad.

Looking over at Sam and Carly, Uncle David said, "Our dad would bring us to this very stream so we could fish. All you have to do is get a cup and go to a cool spot in the stream. Place your cup slightly under the water and little minnows swim into your cup. It's like a game. After you catch them, you count how many are in your cup, release them back into the water and do it again. The object of the game is to see how many you can catch in five minutes. Come try it."

Sam and Carly played the fishing game for one half hour. Catching up with Uncle David was exciting and fun that night. Both families stayed up telling stories about Sam's dad and Uncle David's childhood as they sat around the campfire. Uncle David even made s'mores.

Carly's mom was the first to wake up the next morning. The smell of bacon crept into each tent waking each family member one by one.

"Let's get a move on everyone, we have a cool hike to take today," said Sam's dad.

Carly and Sam could not wait to bring Uncle David on the hike with them.

Everything seemed much more fun and interesting when he was around. Carly put on her khaki cargo shorts, favorite blue shirt, favorite ball cap, hiking boots, and a backpack. Sam dressed herself in brown shorts, a pink shirt, a flower print hat, her pink and brown hiking boots, and a backpack.

"I'm ready to go," said Carly as she grabbed a large stick off of the ground. "I'm using this as my staff to help me climb and as a weapon if I need to shoo away animals," she said.

Carly, Sam, Carly's dad, Sam's dad, and Uncle David all headed for the woods. The group of five had a great walk through the wooded forest.

"We are going on a bear hunt. We are going to catch a BIG one. I'm not scared. What a beautiful day," sang Sam.

"No, no. No bear hunt and we are not planning on catching anything today. We are going to have to remix that song," said Carly as she laughed with the rest of the group. Every so often Uncle David would tell a childhood story that would make Carly and Sam laugh very hard.

"Let's be a little adventurous today, shall we," asked Uncle David.

"How adventurous do you want to be," asked Sam's dad.

"Let's veer off the hiking trail and explore the woods," answered Uncle David.

"Ummmm...I do not think that is a good idea," said Carly with a squeaky voice.

"I'm with Carly on this one," said Sam.

"Girls, we are going to be here to protect you so you have nothing to worry about. Uncle David and I pretty much know this forest like the back of our hands because we would come here so much. You are going to like the adventure," said Sam's dad.

Uncle David took a step to his right and proceeded to walk off of the trail. Carly's palms started to sweat and her heart started to beat very fast.

"I really don't think that this is a good idea," explained Carly.

"It's ok. I promise. Come hold my hand and walk with me," said Uncle David.

Carly could feel her heart slowing down. Her palms were no longer sweating. She started feeling like her normal self when a loud rustle was heard in the trees. Carly quickly jumped back behind Uncle David.

"What was that," Carly asked.

"I'm not sure. Ray...Todd...did you hear that," asked Uncle David.

The group froze in their tracks.

Uncle David pointed to the large evergreen tree in front of them and said, "Oh no, look at that."

On an 89 foot tall, 9 foot wide tree was large claw marks. The marks were very deep and appeared to be fresh.

"Dave, looks like we have company. Judging from these fresh bear tracks on the ground, seems it was recently here," said Sam's dad.

Uncle David walked over to the bear tracks to investigate. As he stood up he could feel a source of heat on his neck. His neck hairs stood at attention and his bodily functions froze. Uncle David remembered that his dad always told them that if they ever had an encounter with a bear to play dead. Uncle David could not play dead because he was way too scared.

The bear let out a loud growl and stood on two feet.

Uncle David looked at Sam's dad and yelled out, "Run, everyone!"

The group took off running like they were competing at a track race. Carly led the group bobbing and weaving through the trees. The bear was right on Uncle David's heels.

"Faster guys, he's right on me," said Uncle David.

Carly's adrenaline was flowing freely through her body.

"Cut right, cut right," screamed Uncle David.

Carly cut a hard right onto a sloped embankment. The group tumbled down the embankment onto the hard, pine needles covered forest ground. Carly landed face down on her stomach. Carly's dad happen to stop because he grabbed a hold to a small tree. Sam's dad landed folded up a pretzel. Sam looked like she swept the forest floor with her hair because all the pine needles were sticking up out of her head.

Uncle David landed right smack on top of Carly.

Carly's dad looked up and saw that the bear had stopped at the top of the embankment.

"We are all in the clear," said Carly's dad.

"Get your big self off of me," said Carly as she attempted to push Uncle David off of her.

"I told you I didn't think this was a good idea," said Carly.

Carly brushed herself off and folded her arms.

"Oh look, there is the sign for the trail. I guess we didn't venture off too far," said Carly's dad.

Sam turned to follow Carly's dad when she noticed she could not move. Her feet seemed to be glued to the forest ground. One by one she tried to lift up her feet but could not.

"Help me someone. I am sinking," said Sam.

Uncle David looked over at Sam and saw that her feet were below the ground.

"Someone get me a stick. Sam do not make any sudden moves. As soon as we get a stick I will give you one end and you hold onto it as I pull you up," said Uncle David. Carly's dad handed him a long stick. Uncle David handed one end to Sam. Her body had sank into the ground up to her knees. Sam began to cry because she was very scared. Uncle David started to pull the stick. Carly and Sam's dads got behind Uncle David and pulled the stick like it was tug-of-war.

"Come on, let's give it all we got. She's almost out," said Uncle David.

The three men pulled with all their might. Finally, Sam popped out of the ground. She wiped her tears and started to smile.

"Thank you for saving me. I saw my life pass before my eyes," said Sam.

Sam looked down at her legs. They were covered with brownish grey mud and the shoe on her left foot was missing.

She glanced in the area where she was stuck and did not see her shoe.

Sam looked over at her dad with a concerned face and said, "The ground swallowed one of my shoes. How am I going to explain that to mom?"

"It was quick sand and I am sure she will understand once she hears the story. Don't be worried, I will explain it to her," said Sam's dad.

Carly looked at Uncle David and rolled her eyes.

"This is all your fault, Uncle David, AKA Mr. Adventurous, hashtag trouble-maker, trouble starter, trouble solver" said Carly.

The entire walk back to the camper Carly did not say a word to Uncle David. Even though Uncle David apologized several times, Carly walked with her arms folded and rolled her eyes.

The group finally reached the camper an hour later. Carly swung the camper door open.

"What happened to you guys," asked Sam's mom.

"Ask Uncle David," murmured Carly.

"Well, lets just say that this hiking frenzy is going to be a great story for next year's camping trip," said Uncle David.

Chapter 5 ~ Ready Up

"Hurry, Sam and ready up," Carly said as she adjusted her headset.

"I'm trying to choose the skin I want to wear," said Sam through the headset.

Carly gave out a loud sigh as she waited for Sam to choose a skin. Sam and Carly both got new gift cards so they decided to play video games on their PS4s. They loved playing Fortnite because they could team up and play duos.

Sam's dad busted through her bedroom door. He was dressed in camo gear from head to toe. He was wearing a pair of goggles and had a large Nerf gun in hand with extra Nerf bullet cartridges around his waist.

"Get dressed and geared up so we can go fight some zombies," said Sam's dad.

"Carly, I have to go. I'm going to go with my dad to go fight zombies," said Sam.

"Fight zombies? Are you serious? That sounds super fun. Come by the house when you are done so you can tell me all about it," said Carly.

Carly disconnected the headset and turned off the PS4. She laid back in her bed with her arms behind her head and glared up at the ceiling. Just then she heard a knock at her door.

"Come in," she said.

Carly's dad and mom walked through the door. Carly's mom was wearing an all black leather bodysuit, red and black bob wig, black Doc Martin boots and an eye patch. Carly's dad was wearing a mad scientist costume. He had on a white lab coat, one Strongarm Elite Nerf gun in each hand, a blue crazy hair wig, round blue sunglasses, and a name tag that said *Dr. Victor Izmennik*.

"Carly, we are needed to save the human race. Get your best Nerf weapon and meet us in the car in 10 minutes," said Carly's dad.

Carly leaped out of her bed and made a mad dash for her closet. One by one she threw articles of clothing, shoes, accessories, empty plastic bags, and toys out of her closet until she finally saw her favorite dart gun weapon. It was a green, orange, and black Super Commando Gatling Blaster. It had an 18-round ammo belt. This was Carly's go-to weapon of choice because it was fully automatic and fired 18 Super Darts, as far as 80-feet, in under 18 seconds. She quickly strapped the Blaster across her chest and opened the camo pack that was hanging from the Blaster. Inside the camo pack was a pair of goggles, additional dart bullets, and another loaded 18-round ammo belt. Carly closed the camo pack and headed to the car.

"Ok, I'm ready to help save the human race," said Carly.

"Play some Guns & Roses so we can get in the right mindset before we get there," said Carly's mom.

"Alexa, play Living on a Prayer," said Carly.

The radio in the car came on. Carly sat back listening to her mom and dad sing. Finally, they arrived at the rally point.

"We are here. Make sure you get all your ammo and your goggles," said Carly's dad.

Carly, her mom, and her dad walked together as a family the check—in table. As soon as they got to the table Carly spotted Sam waiting in line. She walked over to Sam and casually began to talk to her so others around would not notice that she had cut the line.

"Oh my goodness. I am so pumped right now. Did you even know this was happening today?" asked Carly.

"No, I didn't know anything about this until my dad busted up in my room. The entire ride over here he was talking to me about how all his friends were going to be here too. So I guess it is not a kids thing at all," said Sam.

"Speaking of dad, where are our parents?" asked Carly.

"I have no idea. They are around here somewhere," said Sam.

Carly and Sam continued to wait in line while looking around to see if they spot their parents. After fifteen short minutes both girls were able to go through the line.

"Welcome to the Humans versus Zombies War. Here is your life card. Use it if you are tagged by a zombie. Here is your proof that you are human. Tie it to your arm. If you are tagged by a zombie, you become a zombie and have to tie it to your head as a headband. Have fun and good luck," said the lady behind the table.

She handed Sam and Carly each a card and an orange bandana.

"This is already starting off intense. Can you please hold my life card since I do not have pockets, Sam," said Carly.

Behind the check—in table was a large open field with different props randomly placed on the field. There seemed to be a lot of people waiting. There were kids, teens, adults, people dressed like Fortnite characters, and people dressed like zombies. The zombies were the only characters who did not have a weapon of some sort.

"Carly, I did not know what to expect when dad said to come help him fight zombies, but I have a feeling this is going to be epic," said Sam.

"I agree with you. I think we should play this like it's Fortnite," said Carly.

Sam looked at Carly as her face lit up as if a light bulb was over her head.

"Are you thinking what I'm thinking," asked Sam.

"Yup," said Carly

"Let's play squads," said both of the girls at the same time.

Carly and Sam walked around asking kids that appeared to be their same age

if they wanted to be a part of their squad. Sam looked over and saw a group of teens congregating. The teens were communicating using walkie talkies. There were about ten teens in their squad and they had bags full of Nerf ammo.

"Wow, I hope we never have to go against that squad," said Sam.

A screeching noise from a microphone came across the speakers followed by a man's voice that said, "Hello humans! Can I please get everyone to come and have a seat on this area in front of me."

The man was standing in a white, large, flatbed truck. All the people gathered around and sat on the grass in front of the flatbed truck. The man gave out instructions. After he was finished he handed the microphone over to another human player.

"Signal boosters must be found and deployed from..." said the other human player.

Before he could finish a loud scream came from the back of the crowd that caught everyone's attention. Carly and Sam turned to see what all the commotion was about.

"Oh my goodness. They are here! It's the zombies," said the other human player through the microphone.

There appeared to be a group of zombies heading right for the crowd seated on the grassy area. Carly looked up and saw both her mom and dad coming towards her with their faces painted like characters off of a horror movie.

Sam grabbed Carly's arm and the two girls ran towards the trees for cover. People were running in all directions looking for places to hide.

"What just happened?" asked Sam.

Carly bent over and put her hands on her knees. She put one finger up.

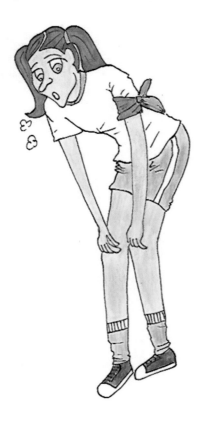

"I don't know but I do know I need to catch my breath," said Carly.

"We barely even ran. I'm glad this isn't a real Fortnite game. You have to do more cardio activities and less gaming," said Sam.

"Hush! We just need to stick together so we do not get touched by any zombies since we lost our squad in the confusion," said Carly.

Carly and Sam walked closer to what appeared to be a tent. The sound of chatter filled the air.

You could see Nerf bullets flying through the air every now and then. Carly and Sam were on edge as they continued to walk and look around frantically. Suddenly, Sam heard a quick whistling sound by her right ear. It was a flying Nerf bullet. Sam turned in the direction in which the bullet came from and saw a mob of teenage zombies headed her way.

"People on me, people on me," screamed Sam.

Carly grabbed Sam's arm and yanked her in the direction in which she was heading.

"Girl, RUN! Don't just stand there," said Carly.

"That's the squad I specifically said I hoped I didn't have to go against, s—p—e—c—i—f—i—c—a—l—l—y," said Sam.

Carly and Sam ran at full speed. After twenty yards Sam begin to notice that Carly was slowing down.

"Sam, run and save yourself. I feel like I am about to throw up. My chest is about to explode. I can't even see because my eyes are watery," said Carly as she panted and gasped for breath between words.

Carly waved Sam on and sat on the green grass with her head between her knees. One of the teenagers reached Carly. Carly watched the teenager's hand come toward her. Her life seemed to be operating in slow motion. The teenager pulled out her walkie talkie, raised it to her mouth, and pushed the button on the side while resting her other hand on Carly's shoulder.

"I got one of the girls and I just tagged her. Do you want me to bring her to the lair?" said the teenager.

The teenager looked at Carly and directed her to take her orange bandana off of her arm and tie it to her head. Carly started to untie her bandana when she saw Sam from the corner of her eye.

"Reboot me, reboot me, hurry!" yelled Carly.

Sam looked over at Carly and dropped her Nerf gun to her side. Her face frowned up. She placed her hands on her hips.

"Look, Carly, you are in no position to be trying to rush me. If you were in shape you would have not stopped running and you would not have gotten tagged by a zombie. I'll give the life card to them as soon as I dig it out my pocket but you aren't gonna rush me about it," griped Sam.

"Ok, ok. I'm sorry. Cool your beans, dude," said Carly.

Sam pulled out the life card and flicked it at the teenager. As the card lingered in the air, Sam pulled up her Nerf gun and fired off four rounds at the teenager using only one hand.

"LET'S GOOOOO," shouted Carly.

Carly picked up her weapon and ran over to Sam.

"Make sure you tie that bandana tight around your arm so everyone knows that you are still human," said Sam as she walked with Carly.

Carly and Sam came to what appeared to be a bunker. Inside the bunker were tools, plywood, water bottles, and building supplies.

"Keep your eyes open just in case there are zombies in here," said Sam.

"Man, this is creepy and it is super dark. Let's bring this stuff outside of this modern cave so we can see what we are doing," said Carly.

Carly and Sam dragged everything out of the bunker.

"Maybe this is like Fortnite and we are supposed to build," said Carly.

"You might be right," said Sam.

Carly and Sam heard a rustling in the trees behind them. Both girls dropped to the ground and propped their Nerf guns in the sniper position.

"It's another teenage zombie," whispered Carly.

"I can't see. If you got the shot go ahead and sniper them," said Sam.

Carly took two deep breaths and then squeezed the trigger. Nerf bullets shot through the trees making contact with the teenage zombie.

"What? How? I just been no scoped," said the teenager zombie to the other teenage zombies through the walkie talkie.

The teenager walked in the opposite direction away from Carly and Sam. A kid dressed as the marshmallow guy walked up to Carly and Sam. Both girls reached for their Nerf guns and aimed them at the marshmallow guy's head. The marshmallow guy showed Sam and Carly his bandana that was tied around his arm.

"I'm a human just like you guys. Please, don't shoot. I want to join your team so we can look out for each other. I keep getting rushed by zombie teenagers," said the marshmallow guy.

"Perfect we can play trios and we can defeat these teens. We found this stuff in this modern cave and think we need to build like on Fortnite. Let's build together so we can have some protection," said Carly.

"That's a great idea. Let's build up so we can get high and see everyone coming and gain the advantage," said the marshmallow guy.

"Look at you having strategy. Let's do it," said Carly.

The trio began to build using the tools and the supplies they dragged out of the bunker. They built a tower that was that was five feet high in 20 minutes. The trio stood at the top of the tower. Their shoulders touch as each faced a different direction. Carly, Sam, and the marshmallow guy stood tall with their Nerf weapons ready.

"I see movement coming our way," said Carly.

"Are you serious? I have a couple of people coming our way from my side too," said the marshmallow guy.

Sam turned towards the marshmallow guy with her weapon drawn and pulled the trigger. Nerf bullets hit the zombies. Carly started shooting at the trees.

"DON'T SHOOT. I'M HUMAN AND I NEED HELP," screamed a voice coming from the trees.

A hamburger character came running out of the trees. He had an orange bandana tied around his arm and no weapon in his hand. Right behind him were 15 teenage zombies.

"Why would you bring all them zombies over here. We were doing just fine," said Sam.

"I DIDN'T KNOW THERE WERE SO MANY! YOU GONNA HELP ME OR NAH," screamed the hamburger character.

"Nah. You are on your own," said Sam.

"Sam, that's not nice. He needs our help. Let's help him," said Carly.

"Fine but you are going to have to carry him because he has no weapon," said Sam.

"Come on up and we will fight the zombies off," said Carly.

The hamburger character ran to the entrance of the tower. Carly, Sam, and the marshmallow guy started shooting at the zombies. Carly and Sam started to run out of Nerf bullets. The crowd of zombies seemed to be getting larger and larger as zombies surrounded the tower.

"There are too many of them. Just the three of us are not going to be able to win this," said Sam.

"You mean four of us," said Carly.

"No, three of us. That dude is just dead weight with his hamburger looking self," said Sam as she pointed to the hamburger character.

"May I please have your attention! Can I please get everyone to gather back at the grassy area where the game began," said a voice through a speaker nailed to the tree next to the tower.

All the teen zombies around Carly and Sam's tower froze first then started to walk away. Carly and Sam both gave out a sigh of relief.

"I literally could see the Battle Royal words in slow motion above my head," said Carly.

"I had 17 kills at 78% accuracy, 8 assist of kills, and 1 successful build," said Sam.

Carly and Sam walked to the grassy area where all the other players were gathered. Sweat dripped down their faces.

"This was the first time we have tried a game like this at this level. The next game will be robots versus aliens and I hope you all will join us," said the human player through the microphone.

Carly locked eyes with Sam and smiled.

"I don't know about you, Sam, but I'm gonna be in shape by then. I'm gonna be waiting to Ready Up!" said Carly.

"I hope so because you were trash today and almost costed us a battle. But we were saved by the microphone," said Sam.

Sam and Carly laughed as they walked into the crowd to find their parents.